RAPHY, LITTLE IN SIZE AND A GIANT IN SPIRIT.
YOU ARE MAGIC AND THIS STORY IS FOR YOU.- C.L.

CARLA AND HER SUNSHINE SMILE. - D.B.

First US edition published in 2023
Published in 2022 by Berbay Publishing Pty Ltd
PO Box 133
Kew East
Victoria 3102 Australia

Text © Charlotte Lance
Illustrations © David Booth

The moral right of the author and illustrator has been asserted.

All rights reserved. Without limiting the rights under copyright reserved above, no part of this publication may be reproduced, stored in or introduced into a retrieval system, or transmitted, in any form or by any means (electronic, mechanical, photocopying, recording or otherwise), without the prior written permission of both the copyright owner and the above publisher of the book.

Publisher: Nancy Conescu
Designer: Mika Tabata
Printed by Everbest Printing in China

Cataloguing-in-publication data is available
from the National Library of Australia
catalogue.nla.gov.au

ISBN 978-1922610-57-7

Visit our catalog at berbaybooks.com

MOTH IN A FANCY CARDIGAN

CHARLOTTE LANCE
+ DAVID BOOTH

BERBAY
PUBLISHING

PART ONE

CHAPTER 1
JUST ANOTHER DREARY TUESDAY

It's Tuesday morning. Just a normal Tuesday morning. Dreary outside, a bit windy, leaves are crunching under my gray boots as I drag my self to school. My heavy gray cardigan is weighing down my shoulders, and my itchy gray scarf is catching the wind and flicking me in the face. My eyes are watering. So yeah, Tuesday.

By the time I get to school, the bell is about to ring. A sound that still makes my stomach hot and kind of flip. I stare at the mean-looking building. Are all schools hideous beasts or just mine? In the movies, school seems like a happy place, a fun place. A place where smiley kids bounce and laugh and play games, and kind, sparkly teachers sing songs and read stories, and, and ...

Not here they don't. Couldn't there at least be some grass? A flower? A shrub? Well, there isn't.

The big double doors lick their lips,

wide open and hungry for happy, laughing children, skipping and hurling themselves into the school's empty math-testing, spell-checking, finger-pointing belly. Swarms of us are swallowed at the ring of the nine-am bell, digested and spat out again at the burp of three-thirty.

And there it rings. The buzzing throngs throw themselves as one through the doors and down the long hall. It's feeding time.

For them.

Not for me, though. No. Nope. I stay on this side of the gate, this side, behind the tree, right here on the park bench. I put down my bag and settle in. I take off my scarf and fold it carefully, and I put it on my lap and stay right here. On this side of the gate. This side. As though the bell never happened in the first place. La-la-la-la-la.

My life.

I'm nine and I'm a gray moth. And I mean an actual gray moth, not metaphorically that I'm a dull, barely there sort of kid lurking in shadowy corners—hold on, wait! Maybe I mean that, too. Yeah, that's me! I'm Gary. Gary Gray Moth. Good to meet you.

CHAPTER 2
MOTHER OF ALL MOTHS

At my school there are lots of other moths, mosquitoes, bumblebees, ladybugs and fleas, an earwig, ants, flies and lots of slugs. Apparently, a spider went here once, and of course there are butterflies—or *the* butterflies as they're better known, like they're so fancy or something.

If you ask me, they're not so fancy. In fact, they're not even that different from a moth, if you really think about it. Same general look, similar build. Except different colors, I guess. It's the cardigans. They all wear them. You know the ones with the colors and the patterns and the sparkles?

All I have is my cardigan. In gray.

My mom likes gray. But she's a gray moth, so of course she does. I'm a gray moth, too, but ... yeah well. Never mind.

Mom used to drop me at school, but not anymore. She's a moth who loves to flit, my mom. It's common for moths, flitting. Quick, rapid movements that give you no time to think, just do. Flit, skim, dart.

We only live a couple of trees away from school, so she would fly me, at full speed, to the gate, no matter what sort of day I was having. She'd shoo me in and flit away again. Mom, in her ironed gray suit and her tiny moth fingers around her neat little list of to-dos. Always with the to-dos. She's a doer. Do, do, do.

I, on the other hand, need time. And calm. To think. My mom says that I think too much—"You'll think yourself into a tizzy, young man. Just go, Gary. Get! Less think and more do!"

I think about this often: Less think, more do. And now I walk to school by myself. More time to think …

When I was a little moth, before I'd even started school, Mom would take me to the park in my dad's old gray cardigan. His first ever, given to him by his dad at the same age. My little gray tuft of hair would be combed back from my face. Mom would straighten me up "like a pin, Gary" and steer me towards the other gray moths. "Go on, get," she'd shoo me closer, "go." But the cardigan was itchy and always hanging lower to one side or the other. I'd pinch and pull at it and scrunch my face and beg, "Can't I have a yellow one, Mom, or something?"

I don't think she understood the question. "Ooh, Mom, I know—a blue one! No wait—stripy, Mom? Mom?" My eyes were wide, but her lips were pressed together and her thorax high. No answer. I watched the bright yellow bumblebees and the red-spotted ladybugs by the swings and I wondered what it'd be like to be so free, like that.

I'm used to being by myself now, but sometimes I still wonder what it would be like to be somebody else.

CHAPTER 3

EH?

Okay, time to go in. I throw a gangly gray wing back to grab my bag and ... eh? Oh no. Oh no. What have I done? "Oh no, I'm sorry, oh—" I'm barely able to get the words out. I've knocked a schoolbag off the park bench—*thump*—to the ground—*crunch*—to its side, its innards spilling across the dusty dirt.

Whose bag is this? I hear a crack. I jump up and my neatly folded scarf slides from my lap and onto the dirt.

I thought I was here by myself. This is *my* park bench, *my* tree, right? There was no bag here when I arrived. I look around, but there's no one here. "I'm-I'm sorry," I repeat to no one. My nerves shake me as though tiny earthquakes live inside my shoes. I hear a flutter and another scrape.

Bits and pieces and homework are flying everywhere. I try to grab them, but I'm so jumpy I can't connect hand to object. The day has barely begun and I'm bumbling about like my dad always says I do. I can hear his heavy, stodgy words like cold porridge slopping into my head. "You're always bumbling, Gary, what are you a bumble-

moth?" No, Dad, just the regular gray kind, and how could I ever forget. A bumblebee glows a delicious yellow. Me? I'm practically invisible.

I grab handfuls of air and let them go. My head is full of gray cloud and worry, so I keep it down, eyes wide but way, way down. Keep them down, don't look up, I tell myself. But a cracked rainbow lunchbox, escapee glitter pen and candy-colored eraser comes skidding into my gray boot. And for the finale, a shiny red drink bottle comes to a scratching, scraping halt. Bits of tattered leaf and sandy dirt smother its battered body.

"I feel you, little drink bottle."

I really do.

CHAPTER 4
MOTH TO A FLAME

Silence. The entire catastrophe lasts only a few seconds, but my head is spinning on without me. Into the silence seeps the eeriest sound of all, the slow and steady crunch of feet onto dry dirt, getting louder. Closer, louder, closer.

Don't look. Don't look. I can feel a great, big shadow moving up and over me, like bedsheets over my head, only terrifying, not cozy.

The owner of the school bag and broken belongings has found me. The owner of the schoolbag and broken belongings is coming at me, slowly, like the wolf in one of those nightmares. You know the ones where your feet freeze, and you can't move? My feet must have known because they surrender straightaway. They point themselves inwards and say, No thank you to running away and saving my life.

My knees rattle and my wings fall limp, as though pegged to my shoulders. I don't dare move. The cold shadow is all over me now as I gasp a final terrified breath, "Oh, just eat me already, Wolf ..."

But, nothing. Well, something. But nothing like you're thinking. There's no wolf. What does happen, though, is quite something. In that single moment, everything changes. It's the moment I'd been warned about all my gray-moth life, the googly-eyed "moth-to-a-flame" one. It's a popular joke, you've probably heard it, that moths fly dopey-eyed and clueless into anything bright and sparkly.

That isn't the whole truth. Only something that truly bedazzles a poor, simple moth can get us off course like that (or "astray" as my mom loves to say). "Sun and moonlight only, Gary," goes the talk. "Say no to bright lights and/or sparkles, Gary, of any kind, Gary, yes? Good. Follow the rules, Gary, yes? Good. On track, Gary. Yes? Good. Now go, Gary. Go."

Gone. I guess the warnings haven't wormed themselves into my head thoroughly enough because I'm completely bedazzled. And like a simple moth to a flame, dopey-eyed and clueless, I drift one tiny footstep after the other to the bright, the sparkly, the off-course and totally astray, non-sun, non-moon sparkle in front of me.

I, little Gary Gray Moth, come eye to eye with the brightest, the sparkliest — the butterfly cardigan.

AND
BOY
IS IT
SOMETHING :)

CHAPTER 5
GRAY GARY COLOR SEEKER

Cardigan, you say? So what and who cares, you say? You can walk down the street and see five of them, if you love them so much, Gary. Stand in line to buy milk and in front, behind, all around you, you'll see: ladybugs in spotted cardigans, dung beetles in stinky brown ones, bees, spiders and fleas. Cardigans, cardigans and cardigans.

Yes. But also, no.

This is no dung-beetle situation. I have no warning, no chance to remind myself to breathe when the sparkles try to distract me, when the sun hits and the diamantes begin to lure me in. I have no time to remind myself that if I don't breathe I'll wind up prostrate, seeking comfort from a dead drink bottle on dusty dirt.

I'm hypnotized. Mesmerized. Spellbound. As though every color of the rainbow and every color between every color of the rainbow is swirling and waving and singing to me, little Gary Gray Moth. Colors shimmer and twinkle, spots and streaks and glitter call out my name. I am nearly blinded. I am full-throttle bedazzled, and I will never be the same again.

Of course, the cardigan hasn't arrived at my park bench alone. The cardigan has arrived covering the wings of its beautiful butterfly. Beautiful butterfly, owner of broken belongings, has now come to collect. Beautiful butterfly moves in on me quickly, its face coming closer, closer, like full-zoom, taking-up-the-whole-screen closer.

I feel small. Smaller. The smallest.

Its wings flap, and I nearly swallow my own face.

Just like that, the butterfly yanks the cardigan from her wings and throws it at the park bench.

The butterfly could be juggling three lions and a hamburger, and I wouldn't notice. My eyes never leave the cardigan, lying in its crumpled heap on my—our—park bench.

CHAPTER 6
STRANGE LITTLE MOTH

And *slam*. Trance broken ... The butterfly marches back through the school gates—huff—across the dirty schoolyard—puff—past the double doors. Arms full of gravel-infested schoolbag and broken sundries rescued from death. Occasionally, she turns her head to make sure that I, the strange little creature, am not following.

Well, I'm not because I can't. My feet won't move.

I look down at them, gray and stuck, and I'm reminded of where I am. Who I am.

And I've never felt more colorless in my whole gray life.

CHAPTER 7
POMPEII

"Oh, but wait, you left your, um, your cardigan." My meek voice barely carries past the end of my nose. If you've seen a moth's nose up close, you'd know it's more of a pinhole situation than anything else. Suffice it to say no one hears me.

The cardigan has been left behind, begging me to pick it up and twirl it around and stand on this park bench and sing out loud. Songs of color and light and everything bright, "Da-da-deeee, da-da-doooo."

No. It isn't doing any of these things and neither am I. Like the ruins of Pompeii, we, the cardigan and I, exist exactly as we were at the moment of the catastrophic event. Frozen in time.

Now, I'm late. Less think, Gary, more do.

Deep breath. Time to go in.

CHAPTER 8
FRIED EGGS

It takes me some time, but I finally reach my classroom a little shaken up. The glare of the cardigan has left my eyes as useful as two fried eggs.

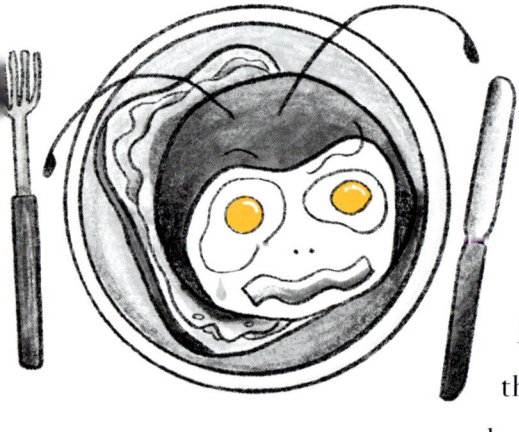

I bobble up the stairs and down the long hall, wing-to-wall feeling my way as I go. My classroom is the small one at the end, with a low ceiling, no windows and one fluorescent light in the back corner. My frantic footsteps steer me through the mass of other insects already bustling, jumping, hopping, flitting, galumphing, wings buzzing under the bright light. It's loud and busy, and of course there's no room for me in there.

"Seats please," Ms. Skeeto's voice hums across the room. We all crisscross past and around one another to take our usual seats. I sit in the shadowy corner, my regular spot. Alone. I'm almost invisible against the gray walls, but today I feel, hmm, I feel a little glow. I take a peek through my fingers to see ladybugs and bees and butterflies having all the fun under the light. And I look down again.

Apart from arriving late every day, I'm a quiet and well-mannered moth. I never make a spectacle of myself. I keep my head down so I won't make accidental eye contact with another living anything. I always finish my work quickly and hand it to my teacher, who never notices, by the way.

First up, spelling. Good, that's something I can work with. Follow the rules, put the right things in the right places and get the right answers. Very by the book and moth friendly. Only today I feel ... I don't know, weird. Kind of like being hungry, but not hungry. Kind of like being thirsty, but not thirsty. Maybe the letters don't want to follow the rules. What if the letters want to make a spectacle of themselves? Everyone knows that i comes before e, except after c ...

First word on the test is beige. Words like beige know the rules, but guess what? Words like beige don't care. They dare to stand their e's in front of their i's, with no c's in sight. This word may look boring, and may even sound boring, but this word is a rule breaker. It's so bad you could never introduce it to your family. It would probably pick its nose during dinner. And flick it across the table. A real delinquent. And oh to be BEIGE.

By lunchtime, I feel as though three days have passed since the morning bell. In nervous flits, I dot-to-dot my way to the quiet of the library. I sit still in the newspapers section, certain that no one will browse there. Crouched on the gray carpet, knees up around my chin, I sniff at my lunch. It's the same one I have every day. A stripe of dried gray ham, between two slices of dried gray bread. I drop it onto the floor and it dings.

Would it kill my mom to buy some jam? Geez. I'm not even hungry. I'm full. To the brim. With gray. Gray socks, gray boots, dirty gray carpet, gray lunch, dusty gray mood, gray air. Gray, gray, gray. Every day the same.

Suddenly, a couple of glowing butterflies and the usual rowdy riffraff following behind burst in through the library doors. Typical sort of noise for a school day, but I come here to get away from this sort of noise. They move loudly to the photocopier. What are they doing? I pick up my sandwich and gnaw on the corner of a triangle, my curious eyes watching.

CHAPTER 9
THE SECRET

So, I have to tell you something. Remember how the cardigan and I were left alone on the park bench? How could I *not* scoop it into my arms and shove it, fistfuls at a time, into my schoolbag? And take it out again. And put it back. And take it out. And walk away. And run back. And stop. And turn. And turn. Again. And squeal. And eventually—*less think, Gary*—walk one foot in front of the other towards the cardigan, telling myself I'll return it straight to its dazzling owner. *More do*—proceed to shove it again into my schoolbag and tiptoe, terrified to my classroom.

All day I'd worried its glow would escape my bag and fill the halls with color. I'd waited for someone to say, "Hey, Gary, what's the effervescent ray burning a hole through your drab gray bag?"

No one did. Luckily.

Finally, the bell rings. And we're spat out of another rough day of dodgy digestion in the guts of the school.

I heave my bag up, onto my back. My wings flap and my tiny feet wobble the heavy load home. I'm hiding something and I don't want to tell. Not even Joey Mosquito, who walks home from school along the same backstreets as I do every day.

Joey never stops buzzing, so I can't tell him even if I want to. Thankfully I don't. I can't even tell myself. Except I already know. Ugh.

What I've done isn't like me at all. It's more the actions of everyone who isn't me. The actions of a brave and fearless, carefree, rule-breaking hooligan. Not me, Gary. Gary with the tiny gray face. Quiet Gary. Invisible Gary. Obedient Gary. Practical Gary. Same old dull Gary.

Pick anyone else and they would definitely, no question, be more likely to do it than I would. Like that guy, Jeff. Yeah, Jeff Slug. He's not dull; he wears a hat with a propeller. He'd definitely do it. Wait, what am I saying? I don't even know Jeff. He's probably going home to make his mom a cup of tea. Or help his grandma carry the groceries. Or babysit the neighbor's flea. Or—

"Sorry, Jeff," I mumble and make an awkward thumbs up.

He doesn't even hear me, which seems about right.

CHAPTER 10

~~ZIPPER~~

And ... home.

Mom says, "Hi, Gary."

Dad says, "Hi, Gary."

I say, "Hi, Mom. Hi, Dad." I scuff past the gray sofa, past the gray flowers in the ugly gray vase that I made when I was five.

I remember the day I made it. The actual day. It was one of our first-ever art classes, and we were all tiny and shy. We didn't know each other yet and our art teacher, the lanky old grasshopper Mr. Leaper, asked us all about our favorite color. We went around the circle, one by one. Some kids said blue, some said green, a lot said red and one very sassy little flea said his favorite color was gray. Everyone laughed. They sniggered and said that gray wasn't even a color. That gray was a shade, and how could he not know that gray was a shade? That gray could not be anyone's favorite color.

I put my shaky hand up and asked whether I could please go to the bathroom. Please, the bathroom? I didn't need to go to the bathroom. I needed to escape the question because if gray isn't a

color, then what do you even call me?

I walk past the gray kitchen with the gray window, framing the cold gray sky. Everything is spotless. My mom is a flitter, but my dad is a zipper. Zipping here, tidying there, wiping, rinsing, flushing, trimming, dusting, zip-zipping.

I scrape past my mom and dad and their neat gray smiles, their fluffy gray slippers, sipping their Earl Gray tea on the old gray sofa in front of the gray television. My feet won't stop. My mouth smiles, but my eyes scream, "Move, move, and NEVER stop!" Until I get inside my bedroom. Then I stop, 'cause otherwise I'd walk into the wall.

I throw my bag down, as though it's on fire. I sit on my gray bed and stare at it, the same bag I've had since my first day of school. But I don't recognize it now. I'm afraid to even touch it, let alone open it. I look around my tiny bedroom. Dark, gray walls. Low, gray ceiling. Gray curtains. Gray desk. Chair. Carpet. Gray wardrobe with my short-sleeved gray shirts hanging limply, side by side, with nowhere to go.

One desk lamp in the corner, my only light. Gray.

Eventually, I stand up and shove my schoolbag into the gray cupboard. What else am I supposed to do with it?

Less think.

Slowly, feeling like I'm in a muffled dream, I put my pajamas on. Bright red ones. Ha, just kidding—they're gray.

More do.

I can hear the TV in the lounge room. Mom and Dad are watching "The Gray Today," a nightly news program for "the colorless bug."

The soft, gray light is flickering in under my gray door. Usually I find this comforting, but today I definitely don't. It's not dark outside, but I don't care. I climb in under the heavy gray sheets and close my beady gray eyes.

    I toss and turn.

    I get up.

    I open the cupboard.

    I open my bag.

    I pull out the cardigan.

    I hold it up, and I stare at it.

    Color fills the air around me just like I knew it would. I hold my breath, move one wing and then the other.

    AND I PUT IT ON ...

CHAPTER 11
MADAME BUTTER(FLY)

Tuesday. Tuesday, my favorite. Perfect breeze, yellow leaves like giant crunchy cornflakes lining the streets on my way to school. My spotty scarf hugs my shoulders as though it's as excited as I am. Orange and yellow and warm. Tuesday.

"See-ya-bye, Mom," I say and I run. Mom hates it when I do that, but I can see my friends across the schoolyard.

"Shoelace, Florence," she coos.

Oh. I dump my bag, hoist my foot up on the park bench, do up my shoelace and keep running.

The bell rings, and like a switch has been flicked, everyone stops what they're doing and swarms inside.

"Come on, Florence," I can hear my friends calling as they disappear through the doors.

My life.

I'm ten and guess what, I'm a butterfly. And I mean an actual butterfly. I don't mean that I'm sort of like a butterfly; beautiful, vibrant, basking brightly in the sunlight and all that. Well, not on purpose I'm not. Gross. Hi, I'm Florence. Florence Butterfly. Hey, hi.

Mom flew me to school this morning 'cause I was late. Actually she swooped me here. I can't do that, swoop. She's a perfect butterfly, my mom—I come from a long line of them. My whole life people have been saying to me, "Ooh your mother, Florence, she's so composed.' It's a butterfly thing.

"Uh-huh," I'd always reply. Composed ... composed. For a while, I didn't even know what that meant. Composed. Had I been agreeing that Mom was cross-eyed? Smelly? Completely stupid? Had an extra wing where she shouldn't? Composed, composed, hmm ...

I eventually looked it up and as it turns out yeah, Mom is. She's so composed. The very definition: "Serene, self-possessed, calm and free from agitation." It's all true.

Graceful. Unflappable. They're also things people say about her, and even I can see that. Mom is unflappable. But me, I flap. I'm so flappable. My mom can take a landing without a single shake of a leaf. Me? By breakfast this morning, I'd lost my lunchbox, tripped and spilled toothpaste on my clothes and boots. Did I mention they're my favorite boots, the dark brown ones? I was really flapping by then.

Mom was calm, though. She said it didn't matter. She said I needn't worry. She said everything can be taken care of. That nothing's a problem. She said she'd never liked those boots anyway (wait, what?) and that she had a surprise for me.

My wings tightened. What kind of surprise?

"Florence, I knew you'd love them the moment I saw them."

I would? Two glowing red shoes.

"With silver lightning strikes along the sides, sparkly ones," she gleamed (she gleams too), thrilled to put them in my hands.

I dropped my headphones around my shoulders and wiped the last of the toothpaste down the front of my clothes before accepting the luminous package.

"Put them on, go on."

My toes clenched and my wings flapped a little, but I tried not to show it. Same as when you yawn but just about turn your face inside out to hide it.

Lightning strikes? Breathe. "Sure, Mom, okay."

"They'll match perfectly with your cardigan, Florence."

My cardigan. Hmm. All butterflies have one. For my first day of school, back in kindergarten, Mom had mine ready. Pressed. Folded. Wrapped. A gift. It had been hers, her first.

Her eyes looked shiny—tears?—when she put it in my hands.

"For you."

For me.

Over my wings it went and it was huge. Oh, well. Maybe it'd have to sit tight in the back of the cupboard a few more years, or even like, forever?

"Oh, Florence," definitely tears, "so beautiful. So special." Her hands pressed together across her heart. "You're like a real butterfly now."

I am?

The first time I arrived at Grandma's wearing it, she scanned my cardigan situation top to bottom. Her face softened. "Okay, now get that look off your face, Flo, I know what we'll do."

Well, phew, but of course she did. I'd held off from worrying because I knew Grandma would have a way around this. Shoulders back, I marched in and sat by the fire, ready for the magical solution.

"Well, Grandma? Well!"

Cool and calm, she took out her needle and thread, a bit of a nip and a lot of a tuck around the middle and some black, white and silver sequins and done. Like magic she had indeed known what to do. Grandma copied my drawing of a skull and crossbones across the back, big and bold, in perfect shades of gray and silver sequins. I'd never seen another cardigan like it. The cardigan and I emerged as something I could sort of recognize. Surprise, surprise. Me.

Mom was devastated. Of course she was. Why hadn't I thought that bit through? Her very own butterfly cardigan, full of memories, passed down to me and my clumsy shoulders.

Eventually, I did grow into my renegade cardigan. Except that my mom's disappointment grew with me. "No one would even know there was a butterfly under there, Florence," she'd say.

I mean, I've wondered myself, Is there even a butterfly under here?

When she's really underwhelmed by me, there is louder advice. "Florence, wings high, no higher, now out, Florence, stand up straight, and out. Florence? And shine. No, like this, like me. Just do as I do. Up, and down, and in, and out."

So, like the dance we danced, I tolerated the red lightning-strike shoes and advice, and she tolerated me.

CHAPTER 12
OH?

Okay, my bag. Where did I leave it? I lose everything, you know. Yesterday I lost a boot, just one, the same one I spilled toothpaste on this morning. When I bobbled into the kitchen without it, Mom stared and sighed, and stared at my one-socked foot and sighed, and asked me how I could lose "only one"?

How would I know? It wouldn't be lost if I knew that. She said that wasn't an answer. I said it was. Anyway, my bag, where, where, I scan the ground. There! Out the gate, on the park bench, that's right.

"Oh—oh! OH?"

Why is my homework flying around?

"Stop!" I yell.

Nothing is stopping. Papers are flying.

I breathe loudly. Volume down, Florence, Mom would say if she was here. Breathe. But my entire bag is upside down. I walk quickly. There, see, my rainbow lunchbox is falling out and under the bench and there, my pencil case, my glitter pens are rolling in all directions.

"STOP!"

Is that …? It's hard to see against the gray sky, but yeah, it is. It's a gray moth.

CHAPTER 13
GROUPIES + SUPER FANS

I'm supposed to be calm in this moment, I know I am. Calm and free from agitation, all that blah-blah. But my homework's in a tree.

I'm up to my eyeballs in agitation. The "Queens of the Beehive" poster I made for my class project, "Queen Nectaria of the Mudhive", is in a tree.

"Oi, hello?" I think I scared it.

"Will you stop!" I move closer. Composed? No. Calm? No. Breathing heavily and a little spitty? Yes.

I move closer again. My wide, flapping wings block the light, and in my shadow I almost lose the moth. Almost but not quite.

It looks like a spring has sprung from its brain, and its eyes are glassy and staring.

I lean in and say, "Hey," less loud this time.

The moth reaches out a hand, all grabby-like.

Whoa! I step backwards. It steps forward. I step backwards. Its spindly fingers are wiggling at me.

I hold up my own fingers in mock surrender and say, "Okay, okay. I think I know what this is about." I've seen this sort of thing before. "You're a moth, I'm in sparkles." I move back further. "I get it, but come on." It's obsessed. "I'm not who you think I am."

I tear my cardigan off my wings to save it from whatever is about to go down. In a hurry to get away from the crazed moth, I drop to my hands and knees and grab anything I can. Then covered in dirt, I run.

This is not the entrance I'd planned to make today.

CHAPTER 14
SLAM

I run inside the school gate and across the yard. Where are my friends when I need them?

Rosie's my best friend, Rosie Butterfly. She lives in the apple tree next to mine. And Buddy, he lives in the rosemary bush behind. The three of us have been best friends since we were caterpillars. Even our cocoons were hung side by side.

Rosie came out of hers first, so she's the eldest. Then Buddy, then me. Mom says I took so long because I'm that forgetful. She says she's joking, but I don't think she is. Grandma says I took so long because perfection takes time. I know she's just saying that, but I like it. Plus, I'm not that forgetful.

Rosie and Buddy are better butterflies than I am. My mom says Rosie's "very bright," and she's right, you know. Rosie is so bright that when she's around I can almost blend in. I've never wanted to shine that brightly. Maybe it's why we're such good friends. As for Buddy, he's a natural, too. "Vibrant," my mom says. He loves to shine. Any light—sunlight, moonlight, spotlight—Buddy's in it. He's a real showman, a classic butterfly. But I like him because he's Buddy, funny and the kindest friend you could ever have. On those days when Mom gives me her extra advice, my friends are extra nice. "Who cares, Flo, so what if you're not the brightest butterfly?" they say. "You're by far the boldest. You do things your way." And it's mostly true.

I burst through the double doors, sending them flying against the wall and slamming shut behind me. Dramatic, but a complete accident. Not what my mom meant by stand out, I don't think ...

The gray moth isn't following me, phew! I keep checking. Wingfuls of dirty, broken scraps go straight in the bin. Glitter pens, ugly rainbow lunchbox, drink bottle, the whole lot, get it all away from me.

A gray scarf—not even mine—what am I meant to do with this? The sooner I'm in my classroom, the sooner I can hide behind Rosie and Buddy, and maybe no one will notice I'm late.

Butterflies aren't late. Well, butterflies aren't, but I am. I try to glide gracefully, on time, soar through a doorway, land grandly without a sound. Like my mom. Like Rosie. But it never works because I'm not graceful and I'm not careful. I'm careless, that's what my mom says—"Think before you act, Florence."

But I don't know, who has time for that?

CHAPTER 15
Soft AS BUTTER(FLY)

I breathe loudly into my cold hands, loudly for a butterfly. I know because the ants standing in the doorway of 4B glance across at me. My eyes fall straight to my feet. I don't mean it. I can't help it. Mom always compares my breathing to hers: "*Soft like butter-*fly. You try, Florence." And I did, once, I swear.

I galumph into my classroom, big and loud and obvious, even though I'm trying to be quiet and invisible. Everyone's eyes follow me across the room. Rosie and Buddy are sitting together in their usual seats under the light waiting for me. Both sparkling like disco balls.

"Rosie! Buddy, hey."

Buddy is wearing a hot-pink hat covered in gold sequins and the word FLY in green puff paint. It's part of his soccer uniform. I'm a bit frazzled and my wings are flappy, so I'm happy to see them. They turn to me but quickly look less happy to see me.

"What? You guys, what's wrong?" I ask. "Rosie ... what?"

"Florence," Rosie does that thing where you talk through your teeth, "what happened?"

"That was quick. Who told you?"

"Told me what? Why are you ...? And where's your ...?" She leans right in. "Your cardigan, Flo?"

I feel the color drop from my face to my feet. My cardigan—and the present I made for Grandma in the pocket. Worst day ever.

CHAPTER 16
SHADES OF GRAY

With all my noise and clomping and galumphing, never concentrating, never thinking, always dropping and losing things, I've lost my cardigan. This would never happen to Mom or Rosie or Buddy. If I was more like them, this would never happen to me. But it does.

It isn't just the cardigan. It's Grandma's present. I'd put it in my

pocket to keep it safe. I told her I had the greatest birthday present ever for her. And that only she and I would even know what it meant because it was perfect. And that she would love it, and that I loved it. How can I tell her I've lost it now? I'll have to go into hiding. I'll have to join the circus or stow away on a ship to Jamaica or wear a cloak and join a traveling Harry Potter fan club for the rest of my life. Or I'll have to find it.

I run to the window to see straight down to the front gate. There's the park bench next to the old tree ...BUT THERE'S NO CARDIGAN.

I flap my wings, and my breathing takes off again. Papers are flying around our desks in my gale-force breaths. "There's no cardigan, Rosie. It's not there, it's gone."

"Flo, it's okay." She gently pats down my wings. "Sit, we're going to fix this."

I let out a noisy deep breath. Rosie is good with fixing things.

"Hey, Buddy," she says, "grab your soccer jersey. Florence can wear it till we sort this out."

"It's at home, plus it stinks. There's no way I'd let her, even with this ..." His grinning face says it all, even though his finger is the one pointing. "You can wear my hat, though."

Sweet Buddy.

"And my scarf. Here, put it on." Rosie pulls the scratchy gray one off and flops her scarf around my neck. "You need it more than I do."

This is like being three and playing dress-up with my mom's clothes. Which I never (ever) did.

"But why, Rosie?" I tease and my breathing slows down. "Don't you like my t-shirt? Hey Bud-dy?" It's old, faded and has holes in it. It's gray with a colorless rainbow and GrayNBOW handwritten under it. I made it myself, genius right?

"We know sparkles are not your thing, Flo, but why holes and toothpaste stains?" He flicks my wing.

"Ow." I chase him with my holey-toothpastey t-shirt and forget to be upset. When all the laughing runs out and the silence starts up again, I remember. "What am I going to do? I need it. I have to get Grandma's present back."

Rosie and Buddy don't need to be told what that means. They've grown up a part of Grandma's family, too.

"Okay, what happened? From the beginning, Flo, tell us everything."

"And that's it," I say when I'm done, "and I ran up here without it. I completely forgot it. How could I?" I take off Buddy's cap. He hasn't blinked from the beginning to the end of my story.

"A gray moth, huh?" Rosie swings her head from left to right, giving every bug in the room stink eye. "And you really don't know who it was?" She puts the sparkling cap back in my hands. Like lasers, her eyes are instructing me to put it on my head.

"Nup. I guess he looked familiar, but I don't know his name or even which class."

"I didn't know gray moths had it in them. They're usually just hanging back, you know."

Yes, Buddy, yes, they are. "That'd be the best, don't you think? You could do anything you wanted—with no one watching. No one caring. Imagine that ..." And I am imagining that.

Buddy grabs me by the wings, and grins right up in my face. "Dressed like that, Florence, be careful what you wish for."

And as though the timing is pre-planned, a big-footed bumblebee walks straight into me and doesn't stop. He throws me a too-late, don't-care, half-look and says, "Didn't see you there, yeah, sorry."

Didn't see me? Right here?

"Basil! Get back here," Buddy says. "That's Florence. You just shoved Florence Butterfly!"

Basil blushes a burning red. "Aw, Florence? Aw, I'm really sorry, hey."

But it's fine. Really, it is.

"But why's your ... and where's your ..." his finger makes circle shapes at me, "... you know, your stuff?"

"So what did he look like, this moth? Anything you can remember, anything at all?" Buddy turns his back on Basil's embarrassed face and circley finger, with his red pen and rainbow paper at the ready.

"Well, he was gray," I say, holding up his colored paper and rolling my eyes. "And a horrible little thief. That's it, that's all I remember." I grab his pen. I'm the artist around here. The outline is easy; there isn't much to it.

"We'll find him. Don't worry," Rosie says. And we will. Rosie is like that. She may be a perfect butterfly, but only till you mess with her best friends.

"Seats please."

We have a spelling test that I've accidentally (completely, deliberately) forgotten about (... ignored). My cardigan and Grandma's present are going to have to wait. But I can't concentrate. Why can't words be spelled the way they sound? Wouldn't it be easier? I have to guess all over the place. All the time an extra letter here, some sort of vowel there. A double *t* somewhere. Why?

Buddy's good at it, though. "Slow and methodical, Flo, I can help you. It's not as hard as you think."

Slow and what? First word on the test is, beige.

Aw man, B-A-Y-J? Do I add an *e* at the end, do you think? B-A-Y-J-E. Okay done. Next ...

Lunchtime, finally. Except I chucked my whole stupid, scratched-up rainbow lunchbox in the bin this morning, remember? I hadn't thought that through, had I ... Think before you act, Florence. There they are again, Mom's words prickling across my shoulders.

I don't have time to eat anyway because Rosie has a plan.

"Library. Now," she says.

So I do. I library, now.

CHAPTER 17
GO TEAM

The library is empty. Rosie ushers me to the photocopier and behind us come the usual crowds and noise. There are always bugs straggling behind us wherever we go. Today I'm stuck in the straggling crowd myself, being bumped and shoved then yanked to the front by an efficient Rosie.

"I've made your drawing into a flyer, Flo. Check it out. One hundred copies, quick, go," and she points to the photocopier.

I like it when Rosie takes over. Less thinking for me, which is just as well. "Yes, Captain," I joke.

Rosie tries not to smile, "What about old Mr. Plod? He'll have a fit when he sees what we're doing. All the paper ..." I say.

"He won't see," Rosie says. "Buddy, go talk to him about soccer or something else boring."

Buddy rolls his eyes and smiles at me, then wanders off to Mr. Plod's desk.

One hundred copies are eventually stacked, stuck to walls or handed to milling bugs all the way back to class. Every insect low on the color spectrum is given a full once-over, close-up, steely side-eye from Rosie Butterfly. She is so in the moment she even bails me up, mistaking me for a gray moth. I've gotta say, I'm scared. Go team.

The rest of the day is a mix of trying not to be seen by anyone without my cardigan and being completely invisible, all at once. Other than my best friends, everyone looks right through me as if I'm not even here. At least I don't have to go home and explain myself to my mom. Tuesdays are for Grandma.

After the bell, I walk to her house. Slowly. No cardigan. No present.

It's cold.

And I'm miserable.

I stand at her front door.

I hold my breath.

I knock our secret knock and I wait.

PART THREE

GARY

CHAPTER 18
COLORS ON MY MIND

Wednesdays. No different from Tuesdays, really. Today, though, whoa, today is no regular Tuesday. And not just because it's Wednesday, but because today I feel light. I feel bright.

After I put on the cardigan last night, I must have absorbed some of its color because today I feel a glow peeping through my blushing cheeks. They've changed from a sweaty gray to a mid-beige. Maybe like beige, I'm not as bland as I seem.

Last night I dreamed in color. Red, you were there, and green, you were there. Yellow and blue, you were all there, purple, too. The lot of you. Blue grass, green skies, orange-spotted cats and pink-checkered dogs (I'm new to this, don't forget). Cotton candy and sweets, birds and flowers, rivers and jungles all bursting with color.

But morning arrived and how dare

it. I open my tiny pen-mark eyes and all my dreams of color drain away. Drabness falls across me like a dusty old bedsheet. Wait, that is my dusty old bedsheet. My same brain that had bathed in color overnight is now zapping back to a tiny walnut. I shuffle my heavy gray wings and my tiny walnut brain to the edge of my bed and slide lethargically out, sort of sideways. Plop.

Wings hunched, I wade through the gray air to choose today's lifeless ensemble. What will it be? What will it be? The possibilities ... Gray? Gray? Maybe gray? I open the cupboard to the usual row of limp, short-sleeved gray shirts. I drag one off its hanger and without looking at it pull it up and over one, two, three then four arms. I button it lazily from top to bottom. I grab my cardigan from the back of the chair and do the same.

And BOOM! What is that? From the musty dark jumps a blinding fizz of color. It's me. It's me in the mirror. I have put on the butterfly cardigan. I stare and let it fill my eyes. I'm a beacon and not even the dim lighting of my life can dull what I have going on.

"GARY!" shrills my mother from the kitchen and this beacon swiftly blows its fuse.

"Y-yes?!" I whisper-scream, knees bent and arms out, ready for whatever collision might be about to hit.

I've only ever seen myself as a gray moth. Mom and Dad have only ever seen me as a gray moth. Everyone I've ever known sees me as a gray moth.

Are they right? Am I just a gray moth? In the dark room, I stare at my twinkling silhouette. Am I?

Antenna back, I turn and spread my wings wide. I jump and flutter, flutter again and try a tiny swoop. I turn on my lamp, come back to the mirror and there I am.

Smiling.

CHAPTER 19
RAPID FIRE

I put my hands into my pockets. What is that? My fingers fish about until they grab hold of ... of *what*? I pull it all the way up to my face. A pen. A glittery red pen. My other hand catches something in the other pocket. A small white box topped with a tiny white bow with a little drawing of a skull and crossbones in glittery red.

I put it down on my gray desk. It doesn't stand out in here; it sits quietly wrapped in its quiet white paper. I start to pick at the sticky tape but stop. I'll open it later, I decide. I put on my old gray cardigan over the top of my new colorful one. The gray feels more like a disguise now.

I'm trying to leave the house unseen as Mom is sipping her coffee at four million miles an hour. Too late, she throws a stream of rapid-fire side glances my way and, "Gary? Gary?" Her head cocks to the side as she watches my larger-than-usual form move towards the front door.

"Gary, you ..." Her head cocks to the other side. "You ... Gary? Gary?"

Ooh, now she's on the move.

I wave a rapid-fire stream of panicked goodbyes right back, "Bye!" and I hurry through the door like an over-stuffed cushion.

"Gary?"

I slam the door and run.

Worth it.

CHAPTER 20
NO HIDE NO SEEK

On time at the school gate today, I have twice the stomach flips. But up the stairs and down the long hall I move, one foot in front of the other, staring down the door of my classroom.

Keep moving, Gary, you can do it.

I feel a warm glow as my feet cooperate for once. I near the crowded bag area ... I'm in the crowded bag area ... I'm amongst the hustle. The morning bustle, for those not hiding behind a tree. Bustling about with the crowds, wing to thorax, antennae to proboscis. I'm not hiding and nobody is looking.

But it doesn't last long. The day quickly snuffs out my double-layered life.

Choose one, the doorway taunts me when I can barely squeeze through.

You don't fit in here, my chair sniggers as I wedge my bulky backside in. One person's bulk, however, is another's glory, so on I push.

And even if no one can see, I feel that glow buried under all of this gray.

Our class project this month is Queens of the Beehive. We take turns showing everybody our section of work and yes, of course I hate that. My turn is tomorrow.

"Florence. Florence Butterfly?" calls Ms. Skeeto. "Today Florence will be presenting 'Queen Nectaria of the Mudhive'. Oh, lovely, Florence, how exciting."

Silence.

"Florence. Florence?"

Nothing.

"Hmm, it would seem that Florence isn't with us today—but no matter. Perhaps tomorrow we'll meet the Great Nectaria.

Glasses now perched between two bulging eyes and a list of names, Ms. Skeeto says, "Gary ... er ... Gray Moth? Hmm." There's more silence as she squints over the top of her glasses and around the room. "Is there a ... Gary?" Ms. Skeeto's brow doesn't furrow, it crumples. "Gary Gray Moth. Are you here?" Her fingers pinch her chin.

I can stay still, statue-like, eyes

to the floor and invisible in the shadows if I want. Without thinking though, knees trembling, I take a deep breath and say, "Here, Ms. Skeeto." I raise my hand. "It's me, Gary." I shock even myself by standing straight as a pin behind my desk.

But Ms. Skeeto has already bounded ahead to the next poor mite; she hasn't even heard me, let alone seen me. "Ernest? Earnest Earwig, up you come. You will be presenting to us Queen Camellia of the Box Hive, let's go."

How can this be? I don't feel invisible, but still I am? While Ernest is gathering his papers together, everyone breaks into a raucous laughter. They are pointing. They are laughing. Heads are thrown back and legs are slapped. They are looking … at me.

I'm not invisible, no. Oh no, oh no-no-no-no.

My chair is wedged to my bum.

CHAPTER 21
ZIGZAGZOOM

In an absolute state, I grab my bag as I run from my classroom and zigzag to the bathroom. Bursting in, I lock the door behind me and claw it off—the cardigan. The gray one. I throw it out the open window. I never want to see it again. I'm not thinking. I'm all doing. Making decisions. Mom would have been pleased about that, at least.

I stand still in the butterfly cardigan under the fluorescent light, and like a crystal in the sunshine, fill the grimy walls around me with color. This could be my moment, you know. It has to be. I'll emerge from the bathroom—I know, a bathroom is no cocoon, but move with me here—I'll emerge a new me. Everything will be different, it just will.

Across the room and to the door I go. It's time.

I unlock it and with shaking hands take the handle and count down three, two—

OUCH!

A bloom of ladybugs throws the heavy door open, hitting me flat in my face. Like a train they whistle by, never stopping, just tooting their hellos and their hi's and smiling as they go.

Hellos? And smiling? At me? Do I smile back? My eyes bug out. Ooh no, don't do that, Gary. I hold my sore face in my hands and hover at the bottleneck until they all filter past.

My antennae up, I stand broadly like a butterfly and smile. This is it. "H-hello?"

No one hears me.

Trying to be casual, I stroll out of the bathroom block and into the open air. I lift the corners of my mouth to show a smiling shape, just in time for the recess bell. I run for the nearest tree and recline beneath it, channeling my innermost butterfly. Bugs talk at me, saying things like hello and hi. And then more bugs say hello. Three high-fives, a seemingly friendly noogy, two pats and a fist pump later, almost hyperventilating I open my lunch. Not because I'm hungry, but because my face needs somewhere to hide.

I haven't been helloed that many times since I began school. This is an exhausting way to live, no? My lunch hasn't miraculously morphed itself into a rainbow feast. It's still gray. We're both very new to this. Things will improve, I suppose.

The bell finally rings and all of us loose coins throw ourselves back in the washing machine that is our school. It's churning time, and for the first time ever, that's a welcome distraction.

CHAPTER 22
FLAT COLOR

Bell. Bag. Fly. Home. I don't see Joey. I may have swooped past him without knowing, I'm not sure. My wings begin to feel weighty as I near my own tree. Instead of going in the front door, I sneak around the back.

"Gary? Is that you? Gary? Good, Gary!"

I scurry ahead into my room and close the door behind me. Mom's speedy footsteps, tap-tap-tapping, trail me. I bundle my new identity into an undeserved ball and shove it under my pillow, then very quickly re-cover myself in the grayest pajamas I own.

Mom opens the door as I'm buttoning right up under my chin. I've put my pants on backwards. Whoops.

"Gary, Gary, I—" She stops. She looks at me for some time. Then she speaks with a softer voice, "Gary. You've not, you've not been yourself, Gary." Her words are delivered slowly now, almost sweetly. "Is it one of those, how do you say, Gary, moody phases? Are you feeling blue, Gary? Are you especially blue, Gary? Are you? Are you, Gary? Are you blue?"

I feel myself soften a little, too. "A bit blue, Mum, uh-huh." But blue doesn't begin to cover it. I've not been myself. She's right. Blue indeed. And red, and yellow and green and purple and spotted and striped and …

In her neat gray tracksuit, her eyes on me for a while, she says nothing. She isn't herself, either and she gently backs out the door. The soft closing of the door is proof of that.

In my flighty state, I take the tiny white parcel from my desk and peel back the paper. A box. I open its tiny white lid and inside is a rolled-up piece of paper. It's a drawing, a beautiful, detailed sketch, but so small I have to bring it close to my face. It's a sketch of two happy, smiling faces in black and white and shades of gray.

This is a beautiful, detailed, perfectly shaded drawing of two happy, smiling moths. I lay the drawing on my desk, but it keeps curling itself closed. I keep opening it and it keeps closing, like it's trying to hide. I know that feeling. I lay the red glitter pen over the top to hold it open. The vibrant red is opening up the gray picture. Red. Red. Should I?

I do. I begin to add small touches to one of the moths, then more and even more. I'm going to need more pens.

CHAPTER 23
YOU!

It's a perfect Thursday morning. I get dressed in front of the mirror and swoop out the back door. I'm happy and bright and I look just right, just like the picture shows me.

Thursday. By the time I make it to school, the bell is about to – oh.

"YOU!"

A voice comes at me. There's pointing.

Is it ...? Oh no. Gulp.

PART FOUR

FLORENCE

CHAPTER 24

THE BLACK AND THE WHITE OF IT

"Grandma, I need to tell you something."

She opens the door, and scoops me in and out of the cold. Without a word of my grayness, she bundles me into her warm house and sits me down.

"But don't say anything till I finish."

Grandma nods obligingly.

It feels like I've lugged my nerves to the top of the rollercoaster, and now I'm here, edging over. No turning back. Inhale.

"Grandma-I-lost-my-cardigan—"

Inhale.

"—but it was an accident and it was the moth and my homework was in the tree and your present was in my pocket and everything was in the bin and I was mad, Grandma, 'cause how can I be a butterfly without it? Buddy and Rosie said they'd fix everything, and, and ... Grandma, look." I pull my t-shirt out wide from the bottom. "Look at me!"

"I can see, Flo." She takes my hands and my t-shirt pings back into place.

"Well?"

"Well, I—"

"No one can even see me in this, and what's Mom going to say? She's going to be even more disappointed in me. And ugh, there's more. Worse."

"Florence, breathe." Grandma's eyes are kind, but I haven't made it to the bottom of the rollercoaster yet. So, no to the breathing.

"I had a present for you, wrapped up, in my pocket. I made it, a drawing, my best ever," then at a million miles an hour, "and-I-lost-that too." I cover my burning face in my hands. Finished.

"Can I say something, Flo?"

"Yeah."

"Firstly," she says, both her hands holding mine and smiling up close, "what kind of drawing?"

Exhale.

"Of us. A drawing of you and me, like the photos we love, the black-and-white ones. No color. Full of possibilities. Remember?"

"Of course, I remember." Her eyes sparkle. "It sounds just like us, you and me."

"Yeah, well it's gone." My nose begins to tingle. Don't cry, don't cry. Too late.

"Flo. Do you want to know what I think?"

"Yes."

"I think that even without your cardigan, I see you perfectly." Grandma beams at me, like there's a joke I don't understand.

I look down to see what she's so happy about, but all I can see is old, dried-up toothpaste. I scratch at it roughly and can't help thinking of Mom. My wings tighten. I flick them out and have another look. I pull at my t-shirt again. "But what are you looking at?"

"You. I'm looking at you!"

"Me?"

"You." She throws a wing around me. "By the way," she pulls back, "is that one of the t-shirts you made?"

"Uh-huh." I sniff, using it to wipe my nose. "Cool, huh."

CHAPTER 25

OPEN IT

"It's very cool. Now, Flo, *I* need to tell *you* something."

Grandma crosses the room and opens a drawer. I try to rub the shiny wet mark out of my t-shirt. 'Cause, gross. She walks back slowly and sits beside me, hugging a book. Wait no, a photo album.

"I've seen these."

"Not this one you haven't. Open it."

So, I do. The first page is filled edge to edge with tiny black-and-white photos. Such care has been taken tiling them neatly together. I recognize Great-grandmother Gladys. "Your mom?" I touch it with my finger.

"Mmm, when she was young." These photos are older than any I've seen before.

"And there, that's you, Grandma." I begin to relax.

Grandma laughs. "Look at my face, I'd just left my cocoon. I was terrified." Lots of other pictures of baby Grandma, her sisters and her big brother follow.

"Why haven't I seen these before? Is this the secret album?" I make a face.

"Keep turning." She makes a face back.

Grandma at her graduation, with her dad, lots of bad hairstyles, her first job, awful makeup and more.

"There's your mom, Flo, when she was just a caterpillar."

"She's less scary as a caterpillar." It's a joke, but it doesn't sound funny.

"She doesn't look at these much anymore. She wouldn't be all that thrilled to see you looking at them, either. But it's time, Flo."

"Time for what? Oh look, it's Grandpa!"

Turning black-and-white pages, I see young Grandma and Grandpa at the beach looking so happy. Seeing these pictures, I wonder what he was like. Grandpa holding me as a caterpillar. Was he loud and clumsy like I am? Grandpa holding me as a tiny butterfly. Was he a terrible dancer like I am? Did he like to draw like I do? Or did he swoop and land gracefully, always thinking before acting? Was he composed like my mom? I bet he was, I bet he was perfect. Grandma always says he was the bee's knees.

I turn again and there's a colored photograph this time, taking the whole page. "It's you, Grandma. But who's that—gray moth? I hope you told him his hat was terrible."

"I did. I told him every day. Not as terrible as his dancing, though."

Wait. I lean in a little closer until my nose is almost touching the page. "Grandma? This looks like Grandpa?"

"It is Grandpa, Flo," her smiling, secret-keeping eyes sparkle, "and what a perfect grandpa he was. Apart from the hat. Obviously."

We stay up late talking, Grandma and I. My grandpa was tall for a moth, she says. He was brave and impulsive, which got him into trouble a lot. He was quick-witted and a fast flitter—he won medals for the flit-sprints in his early years. But he was an artist, too. Well, an architect by trade, but a painter in his spare time.

I feel my heart fill to the brim. Grandma even says that despite dancing like he had gummy-snakes for legs, he did it anyway because she was a beautiful dancer. Then she says that my mom used to dance like him until she had all those dance lessons.

Wait, what?

I have so many questions. Brave? A painter? And ... a moth? I mean, how could Mom not have told me? Grandma answers as many questions as she possibly can, but eventually she's too tired. "That's enough for tonight, Flo, you already have so much to think about. We can talk more in the morning."

But I can't sleep. Mom. Dance lessons? Grandpa. A gray moth. Grandpa Gray Moth. My head. The possibilities.

CHAPTER 26
POSSIBILITIES

I put on a clean t-shirt and a pair of old jeans. I keep clothes at Grandma's, for school. I need to be on time today. Rosie, Buddy and I are going to find my things. Rosie said so.

Grandma asks me whether I want to borrow a cardigan. I don't. She says she'll walk me to school if I'm too tired to fly. I'm not. The opposite. My wings feel like they'll float away if I don't concentrate.

I leave so quickly I forget my lunch.

"Let's go." Rosie leads us away from our classroom, barely even looking at me. Rosie never breaks the rules.

"But ..." I was meant to present "Queen Nectaria of the Mudhive" this morning, all the work I had done. My stomach. Rosie isn't listening, she's unfolding some sort of detailed piece of paper. I have detailed paper, too, you know, facts about Queen Nectaria. Like this one, my favorite.

Fact one: Queen bees have a larger thorax than other bees, therefore require specially tailored suits, hand-stitched by worker bees. Rather than a black-and-yellow-striped bee coat, Queen Nectaria opted for black and white, to represent new ways of "bee-ing."

Black and white. Cool. I made a poster of her, with a drawing. But it was in a tree now, so yeah. I follow Rosie down the hall, why not? Buddy and his headphones trail blissfully behind.

"Where to first?" I ask.

Rosie's piece of paper is a map, a pretty basic one, but it's neat and organized. Her writing is perfect. She was the first to get a pen license in class, even though she can't draw and I can.

"First, up and down the halls, bags, lockers, bins. I've numbered each area to be ticked off." She hands us pens. "Any sign of your cardigan, Flo, and we'll find it. Next," and she holds up her map for Buddy and me, "under the old oak tree behind the art room. Flo? Are you listening? Do you even want your cardigan back because right now it seems—"

"Yeah, I do." I do, I want it back, it's just …

I can't help but think of Grandpa Gray Moth, the possibilities.

"All the dark, shady places, here, here and here. Stick to the map and you can't go wrong." Rosie has a tone. She sounds different to usual and it's making me nervous

"And finally, the office. If we haven't found it by this point," her finger presses hard on the map, "we're going to have all the gray moths called to the office, you know like a line-up. I've spoken with—"

A line-up? "Ah, like in the movies, Insector Rosie, get it?" I look at Buddy and Rosie for applause, a thumbs up? A smile? Nup. Rosie isn't receiving jokes right now and Buddy is still under headphones. All of this seems a little extreme to me, but Rosie is on a mission.

After a thorough, quick-glance down the hall, I move to dark and shady stops numbers two through four, and nothing. The art room is next, beside the music room. I can hear a song coming from an open window. The kindergarten kids' music class is learning something new, and the tune is all over the place. Without thinking, my feet begin stepping to its off-beat rhythm. In the dark and shady spot, I dance. I'm as good as invisible. No one can tell me I look nothing like my mom, or that I'm not dancing like a proper butterfly, whatever that means. I clomp clumsily to the off-beat music.

"Ms. Butterfly. Master Butterfly." Uh-oh, it's Mrs. Mayfly. "What is it you think you're doing? Why are you not in your classroom? Go. Now. And no running in the halls!"

Rosie is upset. She's never in trouble. Running in the halls! She would never. She's only breaking the rules for me. Wings down, her map sags, and she sighs. But like the butterfly that she is, she does as she's told.

"C'mon, we'll finish this later, Bud," and they follow Mrs. Mayfly's pointing finger back upstairs. No one notices me, though. Here, right here in plain sight, dancing like a maniac.

"Bye."

I think Rosie and Bud hear me. Dunno.

CHAPTER 27
THIS IS NOT A RIDDLE

What flies out the window of a bathroom block in the middle of the day? This isn't a riddle, this is a question because something just flew out the window of the bathroom in the middle of my day. Just now, and landed at my feet on my way back to class.

I circle it, looking at it from here, from there, up, down. I scrunch my nose and move right in on it. It isn't moving. It isn't breathing. I poke it. It's just a cardigan. A soft, woolly gray one. Nothing to be scared of, and in fact it's right on time. How did it know I'm searching for a cardigan. Did it see Rosie's map? I put it on.

Larry and Lola Ladybug, the twins who live on my street, run past with a bunch of their friends. I wave, smile and say hi, but they don't see me. I pull the gray collar up around my chin and in tight around my middle. My wings feel cosy. My cold hands are tucked into warm pockets and in the right-hand side is a neatly folded piece of paper. I take it out and open it up. What! No way, it's my drawing!

IS THIS YOU? And a picture of a moth that looks a lot more like a butterfly on Buddy's rainbow paper. Is this you? Is it? Is it Me?

The recess bell rings.

Rosie and Bud will be down here looking for me any second now. What did they even do without me?

The wide-open school-yard makes me feel light and free and I swoop. I swoop away before everyone else comes out and fills the space.

Through the window, I see Rosie conducting a gray moth line-up-slash-interrogation-session and Buddy, the ever-faithful friend, with clipboard and pen, marking confused little moths off a list. My wings know where they want to swoop and it isn't in there. I let my wings flit me to the quietest room in the whole school.

The library. I sit at a far table and lay the folded piece of rainbow paper flat. I like it.

With a gray lead pencil, I begin to add to it. Detail, a little bit and then a little bit more. IS THIS YOU? Well it is now.

"Florence, there you are! We've been looking for you. What are you wearing?" Rosie holds her untouched rainbow slice in one hand and her map in the other, and stares at my gray cardigan.

"I knew you'd be in here, Flo. I knew it, didn't I know it, Rosie?

Didn't I say she'd be up here?"

"You did. You want an award, Buddy?"

Buddy flicks his imaginary, luscious hair back over his shoulder. "Well yes, I do," and he sits beside me and swivels the drawing to face him. He holds it up next to my face, and stares at it for some time. "IS THIS YOU" he reads and he gives me the kindest smile.

Rosie shakes her map at me. It has lots of extra scribbling and circling and even highlighter. Rosie's highlighter means business. It's not like it's her cardigan that's missing. She's got hers. She's even got a new scarf blinging at me. She doesn't have to walk around like an invisible bug; she just has to walk around next to one.

She shakes the map at me again. "It's not going to find itself, Florence Butterfly."

"Yes, Insector Rosie," I say under my breath, but not quite.

CHAPTER 28

The next morning, I fly to school. It was cold, so I darted off to school in the old gray cardigan. I'm so light that the wind kind of shoves me from side to side in flits and starts. Thursday.

I couldn't talk to Mom about Grandpa last night. I really didn't want to, so I pretended to be asleep by four o'clock in the afternoon.

"Are you sick, dear? Florence?"

I moaned and groaned through my pretending sleep face.

She tidied and fluffed pillows around me, smoothed down my blankets and fussed about my room. Peering into my bag, my cupboards and behind my door, she must have been wondering where my cardigan was. I snored loudly. I didn't want to talk about it. I knew she'd be cross that I lost it, but also, I wasn't ready to ask about Grandpa yet. I mean, we're so alike, Grandpa and I. Why wouldn't she have told me?

By the time I make it to school, the bell is about to—oh. Oh.

"YOU!" I yell.

There. I point.

It's him.

The moth—wearing my cardigan.

PART FIVE

CHAPTER 29

Me? Is she talking to me?

"YOU," the voice comes at me again.

Wait, me? I haven't even made it to the gate yet. Just a little bit further. Quick. Move, move. Go, Gary, go—

"I FOUND YOU," the voice swoops in and stops me in my quick-moving tracks. The morning's bright smile slides right off my face. She has indeed found me. I know, I know, I'm the one strolling to school in the effervescent stolen goods. But so soon? I am this close.

I try to keep my wings high and I clutch my picture tightly. I close my eyes. Everything is alright, everything is alright. I'm colorful.

"GIMME THAT!" comes the booming voice again. Eek. Not alright.

CHAPTER 30
FLORENCE

"Give me that, *now*!" And I snatch at the piece of paper. Who does this moth think he is strutting around in my cardigan like that? *Florence, breathe.* I can hear Grandma's words.

"That had better not be my grandma's present ... is it?"

He doesn't even try to stop me, his skinny fingers still hovering there in the one spot. I hold up the crumpled paper and awwww, it is. But all covered in red? And green and yellow and blue. And yuck, glitter?

Ruined, it's ruined, "What have you DONE?"

I turn it over. Maybe by magic, my drawing will be on the other side, all perfect and how I made it. I flip it, rotate it and flip it back, but no. It's gone.

"You ruined it." I try not to cry.

I pull the gray cardigan around myself and tie the belt tightly with a furious tug. I rub my eyes to get the tears out before anyone notices.

CHAPTER 31
GARY

"R-r-ruined? *No*, not ruined, I made it better."

The butterfly is upset, and breathing so forcefully that my hair flaps in her gusty exhales. Standing before the cardigan's rightful owner, I feel very bright. I have nowhere to hide. If only the cardigan had a dimmer switch.

I stand on my toes to show her just exactly where and how I have perfected the drawing. "Here, look. And here," I point, "look, it's not gray anymore. See the red, and here, glittery yellow. And here."

My picture is perfect, so why is the butterfly crying? Before I can get to the best bit, she pulls it away and I fall from my tiptoes into a stumble.

My fingers follow the paper everywhere it goes, itching to get it back. I need it back, I need it.

My fingers follow it all the way to—"Wait!" I stop. "W-where did you find that cardigan?" It's unmistakable. The butterfly looks down at herself.

"That's mine," I say.

CHAPTER 32
FLORENCE

Seriously?

"Yours? You want this, too? First, my cardigan, then my grandma's present and now this? What else? My lunch? You want my pocket money? How about my grandma? You want her, too?" And in my revolting mood, I untie the gray belt cinching my middle. "Have it. You've taken everything else!"

I tear the gray cardigan off my wings and hurl it at the moth. But immediately, I regret it. Is it too late to take it back?

"And—" I shout and wave the drawing around, "it's horrible! I hate it! I can't give this to Grandma now." I shove it into my schoolbag like a tiny, dirty old rag. If it was crumpled before it's barely holding together now.

I race across the schoolyard and in through the doors. "Rosie? Buddy?" I sniff and wipe my eyes again.

None of this was on Rosie's map. None of it.

It wasn't supposed to work out this way.

CHAPTER 33

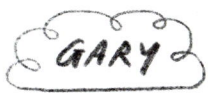

My old gray cardigan flies at me, snaring me like a fish in a net. Hates it? How can she say that? And Grandma? Who is Grandma ...? No, no, no. No, that drawing is mine. The more I grab and grasp my way out, the more I'm knotted into a mess. By the time I'm free, the butterfly has disappeared.

Gone.

I scoop at the trailing sleeves and belt, gather my feelings into a wriggling ball in my stomach and lumber across the yard. My glittering wings feel very showy for such a nervous schlep. I head straight for the slobbering doors. Who knew the kind of sloshing I'd encounter once I moved through them today?

I go up the stairs and surface at the first floor by the bags ...

CHAPTER 34
FLORENCE

"What do you want now?" The thieving moth is back. "Get lost."

I'm cold in just a t-shirt. I stick my head almost inside my schoolbag to hide the tears, but if anyone asks, I'm looking for something warm to put on. Realistically, what miracle garment am I going to find in here? I'm not Mary Poppins. All the old lunches I said I'd eaten but hadn't were here, though. Ew, why so much jam? Mary Poppins would be disgusted.

"Mouldy jam sandwich. Want that, too, I s'pose?" I let it fall from my fingers. "Made it better, pfft, fixed it! Your cardigan, ugh, color! ... The nerve ..."

The bell rang ages ago, so it's just the moth and me, freezing to death.

"I said get lost."

"But that's my classroom," he says.

"No," I speak slowly and use my arms to show the relentless bug, "that's my classroom. You can't have that." Geez.

"But—"

Told you, relentless.

"But we're in the same class," he says.

CHAPTER 35

I'd have said yes to the jam, but I had the feeling it was an empty offer.

"It's true, we are. I sit at the b-back. Also, um. I think your drawing is perfect. Not ruined." I want to explain. "It wasn't finished, so I colored it in."

She takes a step towards me.

Ah. I take a step back. Is she going to turn me upside down and shake me right out of my—her—cardigan? I try to cover myself with my much-too-glorious-for-this-moment wings.

"I'm sorry." I'm breathless with nerves. Would she dump me head first, bouncing onto the floor like trash from a bin?

She takes another step.

Gulp. Closer.

CHAPTER 36

FLORENCE

"Just give me the cardigan and leave me alone. You wouldn't understand."

This is no ordinary moth. Shy? Yeah right.

I snap my fingers and bounce my eyebrows. "C'mon, cardigan."

The moth peels mine from his wings like we're in a scene from a tragic movie. Slow-moving arms and droopy face, eyes low. Very dramatic, more butterfly than moth, if you ask me.

When he eventually holds it out I swipe at it, shove myself in and try to shuffle the attention-seeking cardigan into place by wriggling my wings. I hunch my shoulders and flap it into place, but I can't quite get it.

Sleeves up, sleeves down. Belt tight, belt loose. Collar up, collar down. Shuffle, shuffle.

CHAPTER 37

I can't look—*ooh*. I wince—she isn't being nice to it at all. Does she need to be so rough? Is it too late to take it back?

How can I return to my old life? My stomach can't even be bothered flipping. It feels too sad.

I give the gray cardigan a feeble shake-out and feed all my arms in slowly. I button each button carefully. I roll each sleeve neatly. Not because I cherish the cardigan—sorry, Dad—but because I'm stretching time.

I don't want to be finished replacing the beautiful one with this one. Its familiarity is crushing. I tie the belt, but my arms feel like lead, heavy gray lead. Big slabs of gray lead pencil for arms. If I could go so slowly that time would reverse, I'd do it. Belt tied. The lights are out.

I give a long uneasy sigh and fiddle with my hair.

I'm not sure what to do next.

CHAPTER 38
FLORENCE

I'm not sure what to do next. I can't tell him I meant the other cardigan. No way. I turn and march to my classroom, chin in the air. I'm not crying, you're crying.

"Flo! Florence! Over here!"

It's Rosie. I quickly dry my eyes.

"You found it!" Her arms are wide. "You found it, finally! Where?" Rosie hugs me and jumps on the spot. She pulls out her map and three color-categorized pens, her face beaming up at me, waiting for all the mappable details. "Okay, tell me, Flo, where was it?" she asks, pen hovering.

She always wants to make things better. How can I tell her that this isn't better?

"Um, well I—" I lick some left over jam off my finger.

The gray moth walks in and to the back of the room now. So, he is in my class.

"Um ..." All this time, he's been under my nose. As I scope out the room, I see there are more of them.

"Flo? Come on, from the beginning." Rosie drags Buddy by the arm.

"Well, I guess, um, I was looking, you know everywhere."

"Yeah, we know that bit. Then what happened?"

"Mmm. I found it," wings out, small curtsey, long face, "and now everything is back to the way it was."

Rosie's pen doesn't know where to land exactly. "Flo, what's wrong?" she asks. "Are you happy to have it back or not, Flo?"

They each put a wing around me.

I stare at them both. "I don't think so."

CHAPTER 39
GARY

Like nothing had even happened. Huh. Look at her with her friends, jumping and hugging and eating jam, so carefree. Easy for some. Well not me, all packaged up like a moth again.

At recess I try sitting in some of the same shadowy spots I used to sit in before. Moth-type spots, like behind the art room.

"Hello, Joey," whoops my voice, more loudly than usual.

Joey turns with a start. He's with his mosquito cousins and their

flea friends.

I try harder to be moth-like.

"Gary, hi, where have you been? Come over here, we're playing Worms and Ladders."

I try drooping my wings and squashing my antennae, but they keep springing up again.

"Okay, sure," then I try harder to mumble, "sure." I try dragging my feet, too, and frowning, but it's no good. My feet are light and my face knows how to smile now.

I look down at myself. Everything looks the same, but everything isn't.

CHAPTER 40
FLORENCE

And so I tell Buddy and Rosie about the photo, my grandpa and all the things Grandma told me about him: he was ever so slightly impulsive, a painter and a really bad dancer.

Buddy and Rosie smile a lot. "Wow, Flo. Sounds just like you, huh," Rosie says.

Buddy says everything will be okay, that my mom is going to understand, that that's what moms are for, after all.

You know what, for once I think she might. Mom likes her ways, and I like mine. But so what if they're not the same. An image of Grandma and Grandpa comes into my mind and, yeah, I'm beginning to believe anything's possible.

"You should have seen Grandma back in the day—she had a head of hair like a wild beehive. And Grandpa, he wore a hat so big, Grandma and her hair could've moved in. It was every color of the rainbow."

Rosie grins, "Sounds like my kinda hat."

"I wish we could have known your grandpa, Flo," says Buddy.

"Yeah, me too."

CHAPTER 41

Home time. Home. Gray. Regular day. Mom, Dad, gray vase, gray shirts. Gray. Forever. And ever.

I'm heading for the gate and oh. No. There she is, the butterfly. But this time with friends.

Should I run? Pretend to be a tree? Fake my own death and drop flat to the dirt? Panic is setting in. I try to pat down my springy antennae. This isn't the time to look like a show-off, Gary. You're a moth now, behave like one.

I force my shoulders down but my antennae are feeling festive enough for the lot of us; pat-pat, boing-boing. My wings, too, very buoyant considering their bland attire. There's even some swooping going on. I don't mean to do it. I scramble to get my feet back on the ground.

CHAPTER 42
FLORENCE

❝ Flo, check out the butterfly in the gray cardi."

"That's not a butterfly, Buddy, that's him! That's the moth who took my cardigan. And Grandma's present." Let's not forget Grandma's present.

"A moth, you sure?"

"Yeah. Just a very lively one."

We watch him swoop across the schoolyard towards us.

"Guys," I turn to face my best friends, "I think I finally know what to do. I'll meet you later, okay." I ruffle Buddy's hat and put an arm on Rosie's shoulder.

"Are you sure you don't want us to stay?"

"I do, but no, I'll be okay. I'll see you both later."

CHAPTER 43
gary

Two of them are leaving, but the angry one stays and turns to me, eyes staring. This is happening.

"Hey. Hi, Moth?"

Like word bullets, ooph, ooph-ooph. Playing dead might not be such a bad idea after all. What does she want? Everything has been returned, most obviously the status quo. What greater punishment is there?

"Yes. Er, yes?" I'm seeing stars.

This is too much. Her eyes bore into me.

"Can I ask you something?" she asks.

Can I say no?

CHAPTER 44
Florence

I wave the tattered drawing around. "Aren't you s'posed to *like* gray? You are a gray moth, right?"

Lots of blinking and foot shuffling and, "Yes, but um ..."

The moth's eyes are glued to the horrible drawing. "But um, gray is, gray is invisible. And color...s'not." He smooths down the front of his cardigan.

Okay, not a wordsmith.

CHAPTER 45

gary

"Well, w-what about you? You're a butterfly. And, you like gray."

"Yeah, so?" The butterfly looks from side to side. "It was gray for a reason, you know. My drawing. Till you wrecked it."

"No, I ..."

"You filled it in! Don't you see?" Her finger is jabbing at the paper. "Now there are no spaces here. No surprises, no mystery. And no possibilities! Just all done. Finished," she holds a butterfly wing up high, "like this thing."

Surprises? And mysteries? Possibilities? Gray can be all that? How come I didn't know? Gray sounds ... awesome.

CHAPTER 46
Florence

I think the moth needs it more than I do. Look at him. "Take it before I change my mind." It's not like I want it like this, anyway. "Maybe we're not that different, you and I. I mean, look—we have being complete opposites in common." I'm trying to lighten the mood, but it's also true.

"Maybe the drawing will remind you," I tell him.

CHAPTER 47

Am I supposed to keep it? Is this a trick? What's going *on*?!

"Remind me of what?" I ask.

"Of, you know, who you are, who you were all along. Underneath—" she tugs on my moth cardigan "—all of this." Then she just takes her own cardigan off! And ties it around her waist. Covering her wings now is a faded, old gray t-shirt with a picture of a swirling lollipop on the front. "Same for me, see."

When she sees me looking she says, "It's not a gray lollipop, in case you're wondering. It's any lollipop you want, any flavor you can think of. If it was all colored in, there'd be no choice, right? Now, can I borrow a pencil?"

CHAPTER 48
FLORENCE

The bewildered moth opens a neat pencil case. "I only have gray lead pencils," he says.

Well yeah, that's why I asked, but, "Perfect," I tell him, "I'll swap you for a glitter pen. Rainbow?"

CHAPTER 49

Standing under the warm sun, I'm not sure what to do. Or say. I need time to think.

Underneath. Underneath? There's nothing much under here, just me. Gary. No surprise or mystery. Just me. Gary.

Wait. It's me, Gary! I'm under here. My cardigan keeps telling people I'm not, but I am. And I always have been!

I take it off!

I want to shove it in my bag, but I take my time and fold it carefully and put it away neatly so it won't crease.

I stand up tall next to the butterfly.

CHAPTER 50
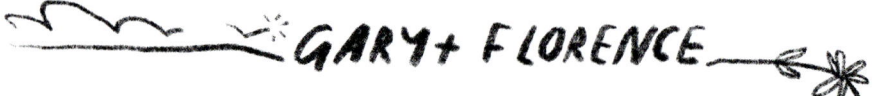
GARY + FLORENCE

"Wait, wait, wait, I still don't have anything for Grandma. It's her birthday." Florence looks at Gary with narrowed eyes.

"Why don't you make her something else? A new drawing?" He points to the gray lead pencil in her hand.

"Why don't you? Help, I mean." She points to the rainbow pen in his.

Gary and Florence draw a new picture. Exactly the same but completely different to the first one. Just like them. Unlike the first drawing, this one is of them, just as they are here and now. No tricks, nothing to change or uncover. Just them. A gray moth full of color, and a butterfly free to be anything she wants.

Gary and Florence, the possibilities are endless.

And everyone feels good about this one.

"I'm Gary, by the way. Hi."

"Florence, hi. And it's perfect, you know, this picture. Why don't you come with me, we could give it to her together."

"But won't she wonder who I am?"

"I think she'll see exactly who you are, Gary. C'mon, lets go."

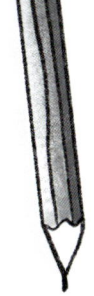